For E.B.
—E.B.

For J.H.
—J.B.

The Valentine Bears

by EVE BUNTING

pictures by JAN BRETT

SCHOLASTIC INC.
NEW YORK TORONTO LONDON AUCKLAND SYDNEY

ISBN 0-590-47073-6

Text copyright © 1983 by Eve Bunting. Illustrations copyright © 1983 by Jan Brett. All rights reserved. Published by Scholastic Inc., 730 Broadway, New York, NY 10003, by arrangement with Clarion Books, an imprint of Houghton Mifflin Company.

12 11 10 9 8 7 6 5 4 3   3 4 5 6 7 8/9

Printed in the U.S.A.   08

First Scholastic printing, January 1993

It was October 14, and the bears' den was snug and secure for the winter.

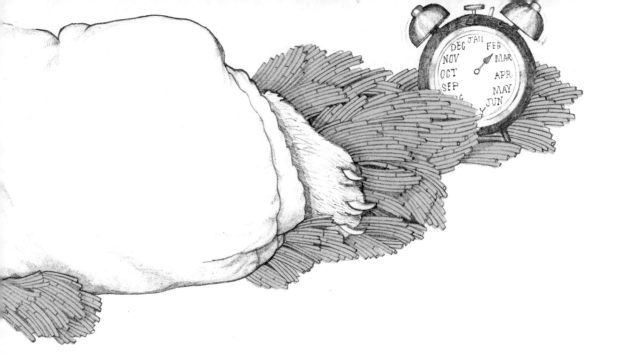

Mrs. Bear set her alarm for February 14. Then she curled herself comfortably against Mr. Bear's back and listened to his snores. It was good to settle down for a long, four month's sleep.

When the alarm went off four months later, Mrs. Bear could hardly believe it. It seemed as if she'd just gone to bed.

"My," she said, yawning. "Spring already."

And then she remembered. It wasn't spring yet. She'd set the alarm early for a special reason.

Mrs. Bear stretched, scratched, kissed Mr. Bear on his
nose, and got up. Mr. Bear could sleep through just about
anything and she was glad. She had things to do.

First she made a sign: IT'S NICE TO SHARE VALENTINE'S
DAY WITH SOMEONE YOU LOVE. She tacked the sign
on the wall so Mr. Bear would see it the instant he awoke.

Leaves had blown into the den while they slept. Mrs. Bear brushed them into a pile and swept them outside.

"Brr!" she said, standing in front of the den. "You'd think they'd put this special day in summer. Mr. Bear and I have never shared a Valentine's Day in all our years together."

Mrs. Bear dug up the honey pot she'd buried in the
fall. She pawed off the lid and smiled. It was fruity and rich
and smelled of summer—just the way Mr. Bear liked it.

Mrs. Bear carried the pot inside and put it on the
table next to the bowl of crunchy dried beetles and bugs.
Crispy Critters! How Mr. Bear loved Crispy Critters.

She had made two Valentine poems way back in summer. Now she got them out of a drawer.

One said:

Red Berries are Red,
Blue Berries are Blue,
Termites are sweet,
And you are, too.

The other one said:

Your teeth are so sharp,
Your claws are so fine,
Dear Mr. Bear,
You are my Valentine.

She couldn't decide which poem she liked best. So
she decided to give them both to Mr. Bear.

Mrs. Bear huddled herself deep in her coat and went outside again. "Only crazy creatures would be out this early in the year," she muttered.

The sun shone through a haze, pale as milk. Crows cawed in the white air. The arms of the trees scratched at the sky.

Mrs. Bear clawed away the ice on the top of the pond. She splashed water on her ears and muzzle. She sleeked her head fur and took a long, cold drink.

It was time to waken Mr. Bear.

Mr. Bear's snores drifted from the den and she smiled.
Mr. Bear could sleep through just about anything.

Mrs. Bear shook his shoulder. "Time to get up,
Mr. Bear."

"Hrr . . . onk," snored Mr. Bear.

Mrs. Bear shook harder. "Wake up, Mr. Bear."

Mr. Bear shrugged her away and turned his face to
the wall. "Just another five weeks," he begged.

Mrs. Bear poked his back. "Happy Valentine's Day!"

Mr. Bear curled himself into a fur ball. "Hrr . . . onk," he said.

"Oh no, you don't!" Mrs. Bear pulled Mr. Bear's ears till he uncurled himself.

She tickled his paws.

She pried open his eyes and watched them drop closed again.

"Hrr . . . onk," said Mr. Bear.

Mrs. Bear sighed. She took their empty berry can, snuggled deep in her coat, and went back outside.

A wolverine slept, safe in a hollow log.

A deer drank from the pond. It stopped drinking and looked at Mrs. Bear with surprise as she filled the berry can. Mrs. Bear decided the deer had never seen a bear up and about so early.

She carried the can of ice water inside. "I'm sorry about this, Mr. Bear," she said. "But you can't just keep on sleeping. This is a very special day. One . . . two . . . three . . ."

"Surprise!" Mr. Bear shouted and sat straight up.
It was a surprise all right. Mrs. Bear jumped and the ice water splashed all over her.

Mr. Bear hugged her.

"You thought I could sleep through just about anything, didn't you?" he boomed. "Well, I fooled you. Happy Valentine's Day!"

He pulled a box from under his pillow. "I've had these here all along."

"Oh, Mr. Bear! Chocolate covered ants. My very favorites!"

Mr. Bear licked his lips. "Mine, too."

He admired the sign on the wall. Then Mrs. Bear ran for the poems and Mr. Bear read them aloud.

"'Dear Mr. Bear, You are my Valentine.' That's lovely!"

His nose wrinkled. "Is that fruity, rich, summer honey I smell?"

Mrs. Bear smiled. "Will you join me at the table?"

They sat together, sharing the Valentine treats, till shadows filled the den and the bowl and the box and the honey pot were empty and the special day was ended.

Red Berries are Red
Blue Berries are Blue
Termites are sweet
And you are too.

And then they went to sleep again until Spring.